A Child's Guide to Paying Attention

Eagle Eyes

By Jeanne Gehret, M.A.
Illustrated by Michael LaDuca

Many thanks to:
• Catherine Becker and Tracy Haupt for current perspectives on education
• The naturalists at the Cumming Nature Center of the Rochester Museum and Science
  Center
• Kate and Doug Bandos for freeing me to do what I do best
• Jon, Dan, Beth, Helen, Ed, Anne, and my writing group, who consistently support my muse

ISBN 978-0-9821982-1-6

Printed with pride in the United States of America
First edition 1990
Fourth edition 2009

A Books Just Books book

VERBAL IMAGES PRESS ~ FAIRPORT, NEW YORK
Verbalimagespress@frontiernet.net
www.verbalimagespress.com
Orders: 1-800-888-4741

At Birdsong Trail, I spot more wildlife than anybody else. I never know what to expect when we go there.

1

We took birdseed to feed the chickadees, which are very tame. As soon as I saw the tiny birds, I was so excited I dropped some food on the path.

2

"Don't, Ben! If you make it too easy for them, they won't come to us."
Why didn't I think of that?

3

Hiking along the pond,
I spied a clump of leaves
and sticks at the
top of an oak—a nest?

4

An eagle circled high overhead.
Suddenly it swooped down and
grabbed a fish.

5

I ran to tell Emily. "Guess what! I saw an eagle's nest and..." I tripped, scattering seed on the path. The chickadees left my sister and gathered at my feet, eating greedily.

6

"You klutz! You scared the
birds away from me. You're
such a pain!"

I threw some snow at her.

7

"Ben," Dad said, "please be more careful not to scare the birds. Come on, Emily; we'll find other chickadees around the bend."

"A pain," I thought, "that's what I am. They're better off without me."

8

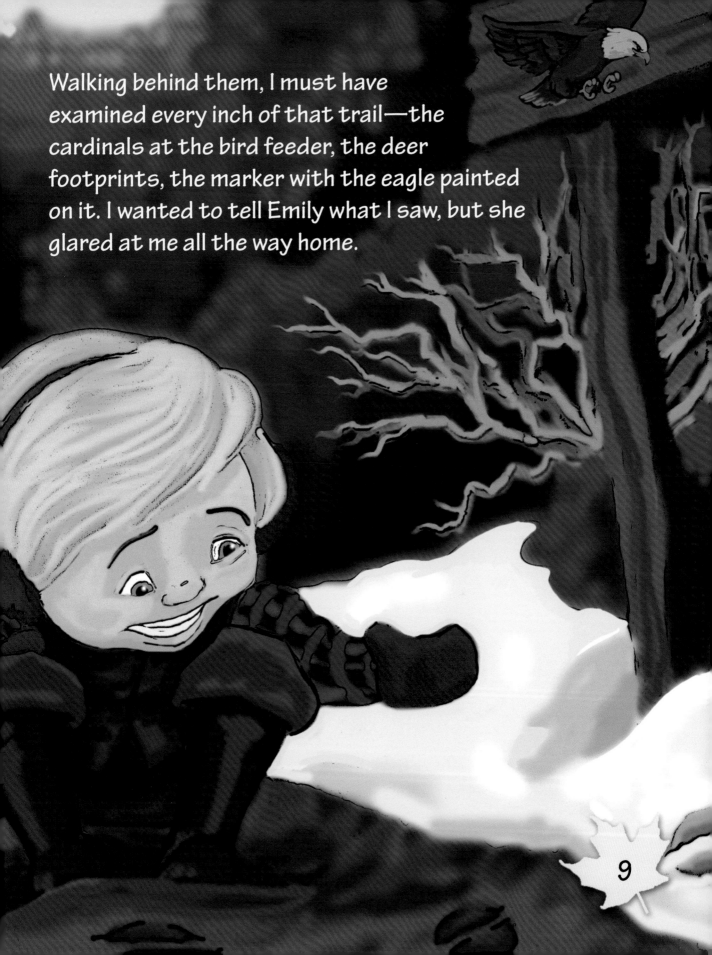

Walking behind them, I must have examined every inch of that trail—the cardinals at the bird feeder, the deer footprints, the marker with the eagle painted on it. I wanted to tell Emily what I saw, but she glared at me all the way home.

9

After supper Mom said,
"Time for homework, kids.
Let's see what's in your
folders."
   "I finished mine in
school on Friday," Emily
said.
   "Good job, honey.
How about you, Ben?"

"Mine's done, too."
But a few minutes later she returned,
frowning over a note from my teacher. "Benjamin
has not done his math for two days. Please have
him complete pages 67-71 of these worksheets."

11

So I had to work the rest of the evening while Emily played. I was so mad I couldn't fall asleep until midnight.

12

"Pass your homework in, class," my teacher said the next morning. I smiled to myself, glad that mine was in my folder for a change. But no, my folder was empty. After all that work!

13

Shortly after that, Dad took me to see Dr. Lawson. She told me I have Attention Deficit Disorder, which is often called ADD for short. ADD means that I'm missing some of the chemicals that help control how I move and think.

I forget to take my homework to school because my thoughts run ahead of me. And all that energy keeps me awake into the night. All this time I thought I was nothing but a clumsy, bad kid. Wait till Emily hears!

15

Dad explained
that I have eagle eyes;
I notice everything.
But eagles know when to
stop looking around
and zoom in on their prey.

Me, I just keep noticing more things and miss my catch.

17

18

Dr. Lawson showed Dad and me some tricks to pay attention to what's important. That night we made up a song about getting ready for school. Here's how it goes:

The morning Song

Adapted from the traditional tune "Oats, Peas, Beans, and Barley"

1.Clothes, hair, shoes, and backpack, lunch, Clothes, hair, shoes, and
2.Clear   the ta-   ble, wash my   face, Get   my coat and

1.Back pack, lunch, Clothes, hair, shoes and backpack,lunch, That is what I do.
2.get   my   boots, Grab   my   backpack, give a   kiss, That is what I do.

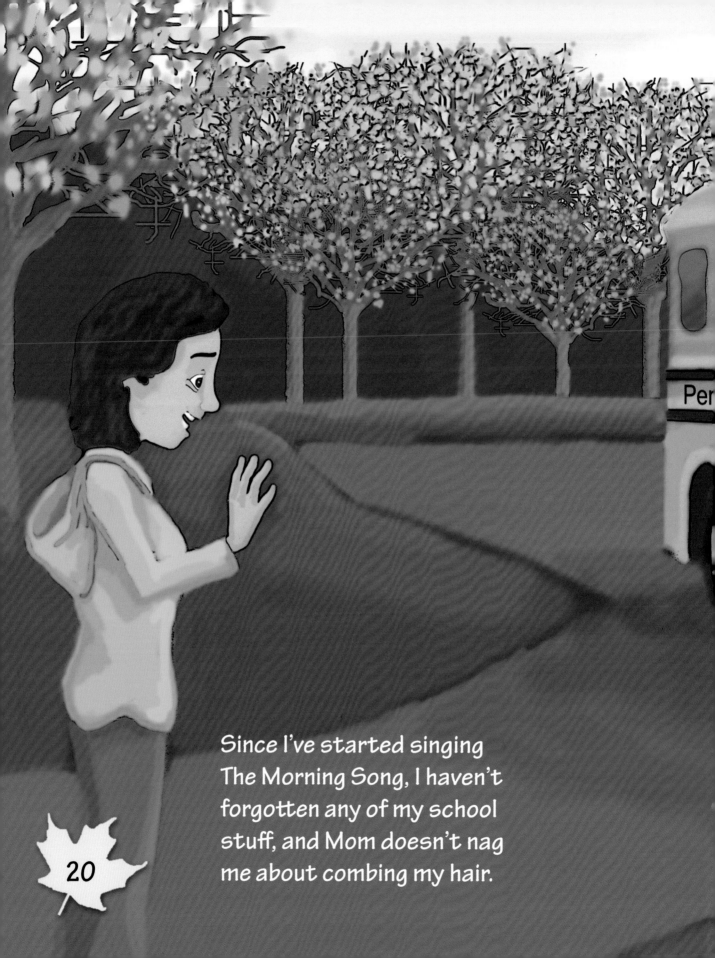

Since I've started singing
The Morning Song, I haven't
forgotten any of my school
stuff, and Mom doesn't nag
me about combing my hair.

20

My new pills gives my body more of the chemicals it needs to think twice before I do something stupid, like scaring birds.

Central Schools

I like the soft music that Mom plays to help me relax at night. It quiets the thoughts that run around inside my head. And sometimes she rubs my feet. Mmmm. Since we've been doing the things Dr. Lawson suggested, I sleep better.

And I don't feel like I'm such a pain. In fact, Emily even seems glad to have me around.

23

This spring, when Dad and Emily and I returned to Birdsong Trail, I took binoculars to watch for eagles. I couldn't believe it when I spied a pair of beavers in the stream!

A thunderstorm sent us dashing back toward the car. Just as we rounded the bend by the bird feeder, Dad tripped over a rock and hurt his knee.

His face wrinkled with pain. "Emily, you're the oldest. Will you follow the trail back to the ranger station and get help?"

She looked doubtful. "I don't know the way..."

I can find it, Dad!" I interrupted. "After you pass the old gate, you follow this trail till you cross the creek and turn at the marker with the eagle on it. It's not far to the ranger station after that."

27

"Ben, I knew those eagle eyes of yours would come in handy. You'll find the way just fine."
 As I turned to go, Dad called, "Hurry, Ben! I need you!"

Swift as an eagle, I zoomed off
toward the ranger station and
got help. I was the only one who
could do it.

And that's when I realized
it's good to be me.

29

For background on the author and inspiration for *Eagle Eyes*, other books by this author, and more, see www.verbalimagespress.com.

Postscript to the Fourth Edition

Much research and love went into this new edition of *Eagle Eyes*, and I can't resist sharing a few resources that I enjoyed while preparing this revision. If you are new to the idea of ADD, I encourage you to browse your bookstore, the web and your public library for information on ADD. Thanks for caring about these kids.

— Jeanne Gehret, 2009

Attention Deficit Disorder:

Armstrong, Thomas. 1995. *The Myth of the ADD Child.* New York: Penguin Group. Provides 50 excellent ways to help your high-energy child — whether or not you agree with his premise that ADD would hardly exist if teachers and parents did a better job at looking at individual children.

Gehret, Jeanne. 1992. *I'm Somebody Too.* Fairport, NY: Verbal Images Press. A novel for ages 10 and up from the viewpoint of Eagle Eyes' sister. Sibling rivalry and co-dependence in children.

Hartmann, Thom. 1997. *Attention Deficit Disorder: A Different Perception.* Underwood Books. An encouraging look at how people cope with ADD and even use it to their advantage. Useful whether you "believe in" ADD or not.

Zimmerman, Marcia, C.N. 1999. *The A.D.D. Nutrition Solution: A Drug-Free 30-Day Plan.* New York: Henry Holt. Great information from a nutrition expert.

www.ADDitudemag.com — This excellent ADD website covers all ages and aspects of ADD. Has downloadable books, great blogs, and a link to obtain a free copy of ADDitude magazine.

www.AskDrSears.com — Good for defining ADD and statistics about it as well as behavior strategies; helpful checklists; compares various stimulant medications. Downside: gives a blanket "I don't know" response to any questions about natural alternatives to pharmaceutical medications.

www.CHADD.org — The first major website on ADD founded by parents; CHADD chapters across the country still support parental advocacy, support, and information.

Nature:

http://animaldiversity.ummz.umich.edu/site/accounts/information/Parus_atricapillus.html — Chickadees' habits, geographic range, diet, and more.

www.birdwatching.com/stories/handfeeding.html — How to feed birds by hand.

www.fairyhouses.com — In the parenting section of this website, see the reference to children's nature deficit, and then follow the strategies to engage boys and girls in playing with natural materials.

www.nationaleaglecenter.org/FAQs.htm — Fascinating facts about eagles' habitats, geographic range, and diet.

Discussion Starters

1. What is Ben interested in? Describe all the ways he shows his interest. What are you interested in, and how do you show it?

2. Have you ever visited a park where you could feed animals or birds? Talk about the things that happened that day.

3. How does wildlife usually act when you move quickly and make a lot of noise? What does this have to do with Emily's anger at Ben? (pp. 3, 6)

4. Emily calls Ben a klutz (p. 7). Do you think she is talking about just this one time or many times? Read what Ben says to himself before you answer. Does throwing snow at Emily make things better? Why do you think Ben did it?

5. When it comes to homework, how are Emily and Ben different? (pp. 10-11) How happy do you think each of them is with their way of dealing with school assignments?

6. Did you ever forget your homework? What happened after that? Does everybody who forgets homework have ADD?

7. How does Dr. Lawson's description of ADD explain the way Ben acted in the park? (pp. 14-15) According to Dr. Lawson, is Ben just a "a clumsy, bad kid"?